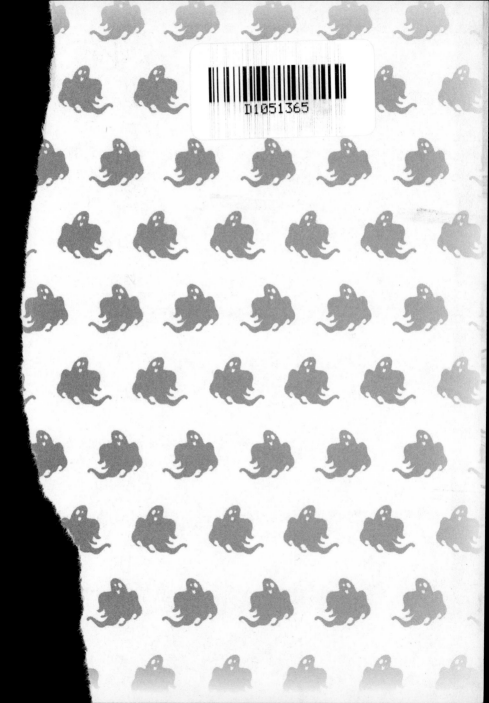

D1051365

DESMOND COLE
GHOST PATROL

A TROLL LOT OF TROUBLE

by Andres Miedoso
illustrated by Victor Rivas

LITTLE SIMON

New York London Toronto Sydney New Delhi

LITTLE SIMON

An imprint of Simon & Schuster Children's Publishing Division
1230 Avenue of the Americas, New York, New York 10020
First Little Simon paperback edition October 2022
Copyright © 2022 by Simon & Schuster, Inc.
Also available in a Little Simon hardcover edition.
All rights reserved, including the right of reproduction in whole or in part in any form.
LITTLE SIMON is a registered trademark of Simon & Schuster, Inc.,
and associated colophon is a trademark of Simon & Schuster, Inc.
For information about special discounts for bulk purchases, please contact
Simon & Schuster Special Sales at 1-866-506-1949 or business@simonandschuster.com.
The Simon & Schuster Speakers Bureau can bring authors to your live event. For more information
or to book an event contact the Simon & Schuster Speakers Bureau at 1-866-248-3049 or
visit our website at www.simonspeakers.com.
Designed by Steve Scott
Manufactured in the United States of America 0822 LAK
2 4 6 8 10 9 7 5 3 1
Library of Congress Cataloging-in-Publication Data
Names: Miedoso, Andres, author. | Rivas, Victor, illustrator.
Title: A troll lot of trouble / by Andres Miedoso ; illustrated by Victor Rivas.
Description: First Little Simon paperback edition. | New York : Little Simon, 2022.
Series: Desmond Cole ghost patrol ; 17 | Audience: Ages 5–9.
Summary: While working on a school science project in the forest, Andres and
Desmond discover a bridge guarded by a lonely, riddle-loving troll.
Identifiers: LCCN 2021062040 (print) | LCCN 2021062041 (ebook)
ISBN 9781665914116 (pb) | ISBN 9781665914123 (hc) | ISBN 9781665914130 (ebook)
Subjects: CYAC: Trolls—Fiction. | Riddles—Fiction. | African Americans—Fiction.
Hispanic Americans—Fiction. | LCGFT: Novels.
Classification: LCC PZ7.1.M518 Tr 2022 (print) | LCC PZ7.1.M518 (ebook)
DDC [Fic]—dc23
LC record available at https://lccn.loc.gov/2021062040
LC ebook record available at https://lccn.loc.gov/2021062041

CONTENTS

CHAPTER ONE

INTO THE FOREST

Ah, the forest.

The great outdoors!

Is there anything better than spending time surrounded by trees, grass, flowers, and all that fresh, clean air?

I mean, the forest has everything!

There are trails to hike, streams to splash in, and lakes to canoe across, and sometimes there are even cool old bridges that look like they were built a hundred years ago.

Talk about fun!

Of course, the forest can also be dark and shadowy. And there's nobody around to help if something goes wrong.

3

Plus, it's filled with wild things that love to stay hidden. I'm talking about bears and wolves and foxes, and the creepiest, sneakiest creature of all . . . squirrels!

I know, I know. You probably think that's funny, but let me tell you, squirrels are no joke! One look into those dark eyes proves they're up to no good.

Ever wonder why they hide in the treetops? So they can rain down acorns on kids.

Kids like me.

But there's more danger than what's above you in the forest. What's *under* you can be just really icky.

I'm talking about bugs! Yep. Yucky forest bugs are hiding under rocks, waiting for you so they can scatter out and make you scream like a little baby, even though you know they can't hurt you. But still. Ugh. They're *gross*!

And if squirrels and bugs aren't around, that means something worse is heading your way . . . like a skunk. They can make your day *stink*!

I guess that's the magic of the forest. You never know what you're gonna find. Sometimes you spot a perfect place for a picnic.

Sometimes you'll stumble across a horrible troll.

Yep, that's me, Andres Miedoso. I'm the one flying through the trees holding on to my dad's drone. If you're wondering who's holding the remote, well, that's my best friend, Desmond Cole.

ANDRES MIEDOSO

DESMOND COLE

And that giant creature with the club that's trying to smash Desmond? That's Ohdor. He's a troll.

I bet you're wondering how we got here. Well, like a lot of good stories, it all started with a simple walk in the woods.

OHDOR THE TROLL

CHAPTER TWO

LARRY

One Saturday, Desmond came over to work on our science project about birds. We'd written the paper, but now we needed pictures.

"Where are we going to find all these different birds?" I wondered out loud.

But something told me I should have kept that question to myself.

Desmond snapped his fingers. "I know! The Kersville Forest! It has all kinds of birds!"

I swallowed hard. "Does the forest also have all kinds of ghosts?"

"Nah," said Desmond.

"Are there goblins?" I wondered.

"Nope," he replied.

"Witches," I guessed again. "Witches always live in the woods."

"That's just in stories," Desmond said coolly. "You'd be surprised where witches *really* live!"

I waited for Desmond to tell me about witches, but instead he pointed to our list of birds and said, "Now we need a camera to take pictures and we'll get an easy A."

Then he stared at me like I had the answer.

"Don't look at me," I said. "You're the one with all the ghost gadgets. Don't you have a flying camera hidden up your sleeve?"

"Of course," Desmond said as he pulled out a flying camera. "But this is for ghosts, not birds. Duh."

"I guess that makes sense," I murmured. Then the answer came to me. "I know! We can use my dad's drone."

But as soon as I said it, I wished I hadn't. You see, my dad loves a lot of things. He loves me. And he loves Mom. And he definitely loves to cook.

But what my dad *really* loved was his drone. He built it himself, so it was one of kind. It had mini jet engines, and a night-vision camera that could see deep into space.

My dad even gave it a name: Larry. Why Larry? I had no idea, but I did know one thing: Larry was very important to my dad.

Desmond knew about Larry too, because his face dropped when I suggested using it.

"Andres, are you sure?" he asked. "If something happens to Larry, I may never see you again . . . because your dad will never invite me back over."

I thought about that. "Well, it's for school, right? Can a parent legally say no to something that will help you do your homework?"

We decided to try. So we found Dad and told him about the birds and asked him if we could borrow Larry.

Guess what? He said yes! But I also swear I saw a little tear in his eye when handed me the drone.

"Remember, Andres," Dad said, "Larry is not a toy. Larry is a very important piece of technology that is very important to me. But you are also important to me, and I trust you. Now go have fun."

Then he made us watch a video he'd created on how to control Larry.

I'm gonna be honest, we fast-forwarded through a lot.

I mean, it was a drone. How hard could it be to fly?

CHAPTER THREE

SURFIN' BIRD

Later that day, Desmond and I stood in front of a sign that read: WELCOME TO THE KERSVILLE FOREST.

But if you ask me, it might as well have read: WELCOME TO THE CREEPIEST, MOST HAUNTED-LOOKING PLACE EVER. ENTER IF YOU DARE.

But signs don't stop Desmond Cole. Not even for a minute!

So we walked into the woods, taking turns flying Larry with the remote control. It was awesome!

Most drones sound like a swarm of mosquitos chasing you. Um, don't ask me how I know what that sounds like. Just trust me. It's not a sound you ever forget!

But Larry was super quiet! The birds barely noticed Larry at all. We got amazing shots of birds on branches, birds in their nests, and birds flying in the air.

"This is great," Desmond said, smiling. "I can't believe your dad let us use Larry."

"Me either," I said, suddenly feeling excited. "Everything is perfect!"

Okay, listen. I have something important to say right here. If you've ever thought about saying something like, *Everything is perfect*, don't do it! Just keep your mouth closed. Because as soon as you say it, *that's* when everything goes wrong.

How wrong, you ask? Well, let me tell you.

Right there, in the middle of the forest, Desmond and I saw something that changed our lives forever.

A bird flew out of nowhere, hopped on Larry, and took control of the drone. And off it went, riding Larry like a surfboard!

Desmond and I were powerless down on the ground. All we could do was watch as Surfin' Bird took Larry on a wild ride. They buzzed above us, zipping back and forth, until Surfin' Bird zipped off into the woods.

"Oh no, no, no," I mumbled.

Surfin' Bird and Larry were out of sight. *Gone.*

And if my dad knew we'd lost Larry, I'd be gone too.

CHAPTER FOUR

DRONE HUNT

So we ran deeper into the deep, dark forest and kept our eyes glued to the sky . . . on Surfin' Bird.

I had to admit, he was amazing! He zigzagged, twirled, and even did loops.

Surfin' Bird was loving life!

We could see him up close on the remote control's camera. He knew it, too, because Surfin' Bird actually smiled and winked at us!

Maybe Surfin' Bird should have looked where he was going, because if he had, he might have avoided the squirrel attack!

"Oh no," I shrieked. "Squirrels are pelting Larry with acorns!"

Surfin' Bird bailed, but the drone was out of control and vanished into the trees.

I told you squirrels were dangerous.

Desmond sighed and said, "Look on the bright side, Andres. That video is going to get us a great grade."

"Only if we get Larry back," I said.

So we ran after Larry and ended up by a river. And that's when we spotted Surfin' Bird again. He was sitting in a tree where Larry was stuck.

"Be careful with that drone!" I yelled, but it didn't help. Turns out, birds don't listen to humans.

Two seconds after I begged Surfin' Bird to be careful, that's exactly what he *didn't* do. Instead, he kicked Larry off the branch. And that drone crash-landed into a bush . . . on the other side of the river.

I tried the remote control, but the bush had snagged Larry.

Then I turned to Desmond. He was my only hope. "Do you have a boat hidden somewhere? We need to get across the river!"

Desmond checked his pockets, and for a second I thought maybe he *did* have a boat.

But he shook his head. "Aw man, the one day I leave my boat at home! But we could take that bridge over there."

Desmond pointed toward a stone bridge that stretched across the river. "Yes!" I exclaimed.

Then I ran over to make sure it was real, and it was! This was too good to be true!

Now, if Desmond and I had stopped to think about it, we *never* would have crossed that bridge. Seriously, it looked like something straight out of a fairy tale . . . and not one of the happy ones!

Yep, if we'd stopped to think at all, we would have wondered why there was a creepy old bridge out there in the middle of nowhere.

But we didn't stop to think about it. We ran to that bridge at full speed.

We had no choice. Larry needed our help. And I needed to not be in trouble!

As soon as we stepped on the bridge, that's when we heard it.

It sounded like a long, low growl. We froze in place.

"I'm guessing that's not your stomach," Desmond whispered.

It wasn't.

Then the low growl turned into a loud *rumble* that shook the stone bridge. The whole forest started to

shake too. The trees swayed, and the birds flew off with loud caws. They knew something bad was about to happen. And they were right!

The drone hunt was over. But the troll toll had begun!

CHAPTER FIVE

A TROLL LOT OF TROUBLE

First thing was first. Desmond and I got off the bridge as fast as we could. But that didn't stop the growling and the rumbling.

In fact, it got louder. That's when we noticed a shadow moving under the bridge!

I hoped my eyes were playing tricks on me, but talk about wishful thinking!

Here's what we saw: a giant hand ... attached to a giant arm ... attached to a giant body ... of a giant *troll*!

My mouth dropped open, but no sound came out.

Desmond didn't have that problem.

"Hey, Andres," he said. "Remember when you asked me what else lived in the Kersville Forest? We can add trolls to the list."

And he wasn't lying. Standing right there beside the bridge really *was* a troll. And he was a *big* one!

The troll slowly crawled onto the bridge and blocked our path with a giant wooden club.

I swallowed hard and stepped backward.

Desmond had something different in mind. He stepped *closer to the troll.*

"Hi there," he said cheerfully. "My name is Desmond, and this is my friend Andres. We didn't mean to wake you. We just need to cross the bridge to get our drone, and then we'll be out of your hair—um, I mean, then we can go home."

The troll stared at us, but he didn't budge.

After a long silence, I whispered to Desmond, "Maybe he only speaks troll."

"Ohdor speak everything," the troll boomed. "Ohdor speak bird, ghoul, even squirrel."

His voice was so deep that it made the inside of my chest shake.

Ohdor continued, "To cross bridge, you answer three riddles."

"Riddles?" I asked. "Um, are they hard?"

"Yes!" the troll roared. "Riddles very hard!"

Desmond and I looked at each other with wide eyes. We had to get to the other side of that bridge.

"What happens if we get them wrong?" Desmond asked Ohdor.

Honestly, I didn't want to know the answer to that question. I knew I wasn't going to like it.

That was when Ohdor smashed his club onto the ground. The vibration made us bounce in the air and land on our butts.

"Wrong answer gets smashed," Ohdor declared.

Yep, see, I didn't want the answer to that question.

CHAPTER SIX

THE ANSWER IS GHOST

Desmond and I stared at each other, not sure what to do next.

And Ohdor? He was standing there breathing heavily.

"Andres, I have to ask," Desmond said. "Is Larry really *that* important to your dad?"

"Yeah," I replied, because it was true.

So we turned to face Ohdor. There was no other choice.

That was when I heard whistling. *Who else would be this deep in the woods?*

Then we saw a glow in the trees, and suddenly I knew that whistle. It was the same whistle that kept me up at night sometimes. It was Zax, the ghost who lives with me.

Yep, I have a ghost in my house. (Keep up with me! Zax is in a lot of my stories, and most of the time he's a big help.)

"Zax!" we called out. "Over here!"
The ghost floated toward us holding a basket filled with old shoes.

"Hey, guys!" he said. "Are you searching for lost shoes too? It's the perfect time of year!"

"Uh, no," Desmond said as he secretly pointed to Ohdor.

But Zax didn't notice the troll. He just saw the bridge.

"Oh, great idea!" Zax said happily. "There's got to be more lost shoes on the other side of the river!"

And before we could stop him, Zax floated right up to the troll. *Bad move, Zax!*

"To cross bridge, you answer three riddles," Ohdor demanded.

"Sure thing, friend," Zax said. "Ask away!"

"What has to be broken before you can use it?" Ohdor asked in that deep voice.

"Oh, that's easy," Zax responded. "A ghost."

"Wrong!" roared Ohdor. "Riddle two: What is lighter than feather, but even strongest troll in world cannot hold more than five minutes?"

Zax winked at us and said, "Oh, I definitely got this one. It's a ghost."

"Wrong!" Ohdor roared again, and this time we all felt the breeze from his foul breath.

Whoa. No wonder his name was Ohdor! His breath had super stink!

"Zax!" I yelled. "Stop!"

But Zax just waved back and gave us his goofy ghost smile.

I shook my head. No matter how much time we spent together, I was never ever going to understand ghosts!

"Last riddle," Ohdor boomed. "The more of this there is, the less you see. What it is?"

Zax let out a chuckle. "This is the easiest one. The answer is . . . a ghost!"

And with that, Ohdor slammed his club down—right on top of Zax!

CHAPTER SEVEN

SPLAT!

If you've never seen a troll smash a ghost, consider yourself lucky!

I tried to look away, but Ohdor brought that club down faster than lightning and with so much power it left a giant dent in the stone bridge.

CRACK!

All the shoes Zax had been collecting scattered everywhere.

And don't ask me why Zax was collecting shoes in a forest. Like I said, I really didn't understand ghosts.

But I *did* understand one thing about ghosts: They can move through solid objects . . . like Ohdor's club!

Yep, Zax slipped through that thing like air. In fact, he was still floating on the bridge like nothing happened.

Ohdor looked surprised. "Why you no splat?" he asked angrily.

"Buddy, I'm a ghost," said Zax. "I can float through walls. Your silly little club can't do anything to me. Go ahead. Try again."

And Ohdor did! He brought his club down three times. **WHAM! WHAM! WHAM!** But each time, Zax just smiled back at him the way only ghosts can do.

"See?" Zax said. "Now, I really need to get back to my shoe search before all the good ones are taken."

Zax gathered his shoes and waved goodbye to me and Desmond. Then he floated across the bridge, right past Ohdor.

"I'm glad Zax didn't get hurt," Desmond said.

"Yeah," I agreed. "But we still have our Larry problem."

No matter how hard I thought, this bridge was the only good way to get across the river.

I mean I came up with plenty of *bad* ways. Like, building a ramp to jump the river with our bikes. Or tying a bunch of balloons to lawn chairs to float across the river.

Or making a catapult to throw me over to the other side.

But none of those ideas would work. Plus, they were all super dangerous.

In other words, we had to deal with Ohdor and his riddles . . . and his club!

Desmond marched up to the bridge first and said, "My turn, Ohdor. Ask me your riddles so I can cross the bridge and get Larry back for my best friend."

"Desmond, don't!" I begged.

But when Desmond wanted to do something, he did it!

Ohdor smiled a creepy troll smile and asked, "What has to be broken before you can use it?"

"An egg," Desmond said confidently. "You have to break an egg to use it."

The troll looked surprised. "Correct. But you never get next one. What is lighter than feather, but even strongest troll cannot hold for more than five minutes?"

I held my breath, hoping Desmond would know the right answer. And that's when I realized . . . *I* knew the right answer!

"Your breath!" I shouted, running next to Desmond on the bridge. "Breath is lighter than a feather, but even the strongest troll, or kid, can't hold it for too long."

"Correct!" said Ohdor again. "You good at riddles. Ohdor impressed. But next one impossible. Ohdor will crush you."

"Just give us the riddle," Desmond demanded. "With Andres by my side, we can do anything."

I smiled because Desmond was right.

"Last riddle," Ohdor boomed. "The more of this there is, the less you see. What it is?"

Desmond was thinking hard, but all I could do was stare at Ohdor's club. If we didn't solve this riddle, we were going to get smashed into dust.

And if Ohdor didn't smash us, my parents would ground me into dust for coming home without Larry *and* for being out this late.

It was starting to get dark.

And that's when it hit me! (The answer . . . not the club. Duh!)

"Darkness," I blurted out. "The more darkness there is, the less you see! Because it's hard to see in the dark!"

"Correct!" Ohdor announced, smiling. "You very good at riddles, tiny human. You may both pass."

He put down his club and stepped aside.

Desmond slapped me on my back and said, "That. Was. Awesome!"

"It was, right?" I said as we started across the bridge. "But come on, Desmond. You knew all the answers already, didn't you? That's why you took on the troll, right?"

"Nope," admitted Desmond. "I knew the first answer, but I was just going to wing it for the other two."

Wow, that was hard to believe. Even though we were up against a troll holding a club, Desmond still wanted to help me. Luckily, we worked together and beat that troll at his own game.

I guess that's what best friends do!

CHAPTER EIGHT

THE LONELY TROLL

Back at my house, Desmond and I went right to work on our project.

We plugged Larry into the computer and downloaded all the video footage we had taken.

There were tons of birds, and we had so many pictures!

We had flying shots. We had nest shots. We even had a shot of a baby bird hatching from an egg. It was amazing!

But the coolest thing we got on the video was Surfin' Bird. Desmond and I laughed so hard watching him.

"Do you think we'll get a good grade?" I asked.

"This should get the secret grade that teachers give for stuff that's better than an A-plus," he replied.

Even Larry's crash was epic! The video was almost worth having to deal with an angry troll just to get it.

Speaking of that troll, guess what? Larry didn't stop recording after the crash. So our whole adventure was

recorded—me and Desmond on the bridge, Ohdor and his club, and even Zax and his shoes!

Watching it was actually funny, especially when Ohdor tried to bonk Zax.

But now, we saw something we hadn't noticed before. After Desmond and I solved the riddles and walked away from Ohdor, the saddest look came over his face. He even waved goodbye to us as we crossed the bridge.

But we didn't see it. We totally ignored him . . . probably because we were excited to have survived!

Desmond and I watched as Ohdor crawled back under the bridge and sat there with tears in his eyes.

We even heard him muttering, "Ohdor sad. Ohdor have no friends to play riddles with. Tiny humans were fun . . . and smart. Maybe tiny humans come back and play again."

Desmond stopped the video and gave me a look. "You know what this means, right?"

"Dude, a sad troll is still a *troll*," I said. "And a troll can still club us over the head if we answer those riddles wrong."

"Don't you see?" Desmond asked. "Ohdor is a troll, so he thinks he has to play rough because that's how trolls learn to play. Here, watch it again."

This time even I could see that when we answered the final riddle, Ohdor actually looked happy . . . until we left. Until he was alone.

Suddenly I was feeling sorry for a troll who had tried to crush me to a pulp. Living in Kersville was definitely changing me.

"What can we do, Desmond?" I asked. "We got lucky today with Ohdor's riddles. If we go back, we might get flattened into pancakes. And I don't want to be a pancake!"

"Don't worry. I've got an idea," said Desmond with a smile.

Oh boy. A Desmond Cole idea. That's *exactly* what I was worried about.

CHAPTER NINE

TROLL-LA-LA

The next day at school felt normal.

We presented our bird project in class, and we totally aced it, just like we thought.

The whole class was cracking up at our Surfin' Bird video, even our teacher!

I had almost forgotten about Desmond's troll plan. I wondered if he'd forgotten about it too. But who was I kidding. Desmond *never* forgot anything!

Because when school was over, Desmond turned to me and said, "Okay, let's go visit Ohdor!"

"Wh-wh-what?" I asked.

Before I knew it, we were back in the Kersville Forest, heading to the creepy stone bridge.

When we got there, Desmond pulled Larry out of his backpack. "Here, hold this."

"What?" I screeched. "You brought Larry back here? We barely escaped with him last time!"

"Trust me, Andres," Desmond said. "That Surfin' Bird gave me an idea."

Then he pulled out a book I'd never seen before.

"What's that?" I asked.

Desmond smiled and held it up for me to see. "It's a book of riddles!"

I held Larry as we stepped onto Ohdor's bridge. The giant troll lumbered out from under the bridge, carrying his club. But this time, he looked happy to see us.

"To cross bridge, you answer three riddles," Ohdor said.

I looked over at Desmond and whispered, "Last chance. Are you sure this is a good idea?"

"It's the best idea I've ever had," Desmond replied. Then he turned to Ohdor and said, "Okay, what's the first riddle?"

Ohdor cleared his throat and boomed, "What not speak until spoken to?"

"An echo," Desmond responded right away.

I held my breath and kept my eyes on Ohdor's club.

"Correct," said Ohdor. "Second riddle . . . What has one eye but not see?"

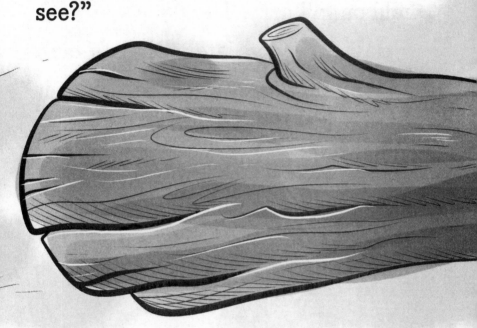

"A needle!" Desmond replied.

Ohdor nodded. "Correct. Now, last riddle . . . What has head and tail but no body?"

"Uh-oh," said Desmond. "Um . . . uh . . . Andres, this is a good time to hold on to Larry. Tight!"

Half a second later, Ohdor's club was swinging toward me, but it missed. Because I was flying through the air! And no, I hadn't become a superhero or anything.

I was hanging on to Larry for dear life.

Desmond used the remote control to bring me back down. Then he grabbed my legs, and we lifted off as Ohdor tried to crush him, too.

Desmond and I zoomed through the air as Ohdor swatted his club at us like we were flies.

That's when Desmond screamed, "I know the answer to the riddle! It's . . . A GHOST!"

Ohdor stopped and looked confused. Then he said, "Correct."

Desmond landed us just in time. My pants were probably a second away from falling down, and I did *not* want to have that happen.

"Dude! How did you know all the answers to those riddles?" I asked Desmond.

He held up the riddle book again. "Easy. I memorized every page! So when Ohdor asked the questions, I'd be ready. And in case I didn't know one, I asked your dad if we could borrow Larry again."

Then Desmond turned back to our troll friend.

"Okay, Ohdor," Desmond said. "We need to talk."

CHAPTER TEN

TROLL-VIA NIGHT

You know what? I used to think trolls just loved protecting bridges and smashing things with their clubs. But that's not true!

It turns out, trolls just love riddles!

Desmond was the one who figured that out.

We just needed to teach Ohdor that it wasn't nice to smash anyone who got the riddles wrong.

And let me tell you, that wasn't easy. It took a long time and a lot

of club smashes. Luckily, we had Zax help us since everything goes through him.

Eventually, Ohdor found the kind way to play.

Then Desmond put his bigger plan into motion. He started a trivia night for kids by the old stone bridge in the Kersville Forest.

And it was a hit! All the kids from town came out with a picnic dinner, and they took turns answering Ohdor's riddles. The winner got to cross the bridge, where there was always a prize.

What kind of prize? Well, you'll never guess, so I'll just tell you. Cupcakes.

And not just any cupcakes. I'm talking troll-size cupcakes that Ohdor baked himself!

Yep, trolls love baking almost as much as they love riddles or smashing things. And trust me when I tell you that when it comes to troll cupcakes, bigger means better!

That's how Troll-via Night began, and it's still going on today. So if you're ever in the Kersville Forest, try solving some of Ohdor's riddles!

I hear Surfin' Bird shows up too, every now and then. But if you ask me, he's not there for riddles and cupcakes. Knowing him, he's just waiting for another chance to hop on Larry and show off those cool surfing tricks everybody loves!